In Level 0, **Book 1**
previous books, as

Special featur

Phonically decodable text
builds reading confidence

Short sentences with
simple language

Repetition of
sounds in
different words

Some children were running
near the river. One of them fell in!

Help! Help!
I can not swim!

Story Words
Can you match these words
to the pictures?

children
river
ring
dog
shook
black
brown

Tricky Words
These tricky words are in the story
you have just read. They cannot
be sounded out. Can you memorize
them and read them super fast?

some   out
were   what
one   when
do
there

Summary page to
reinforce learning

Practice of words that
cannot be sounded out

Phonics and Book Banding Consultant: Kate Ruttle

LADYBIRD BOOKS

UK | USA | Canada | Ireland | Australia
India | New Zealand | South Africa

Ladybird Books is part of the Penguin Random House group of companies
whose addresses can be found at global.penguinrandomhouse.com.

www.penguin.co.uk www.puffin.co.uk www.ladybird.co.uk

A version of this book was previously published as
Wow, Wowzer – Ladybird I'm Ready for Phonics: Level 10, 2014
This edition published 2018
001

Printed in China

A CIP catalogue record for this book is available from the British Library

ISBN: 978–0–241–31261–2

All correspondence to
Ladybird Books
Penguin Random House Children's
80 Strand, London WC2R 0RL

The River Dog

Written by Monica Hughes
Illustrated by Ian Cunliffe

Some children were running near the river. One of them fell in!

6

There was a ring on the
river bank. Jim grabbed it
and tossed it into the river.

The ring floated in the river,
but it was too far for Janet
to get it.

Help! Help!
I am sinking!

Just then, a big black and
brown dog ran up.

It was Wowzer!

The children were afraid of
the dog, but they did not need
to be. Wowzer was a clever dog.
He did not bark or growl.

Wowzer did not wait. He jumped
into the river.

He swam to the ring and
tugged it across to Janet.

Janet held on to the ring.

Wowzer tugged the ring and
Janet back to the river bank.

The children helped Janet out of the river. What do you think Wowzer did when he got out?

He just shook himself and then ran off.

Story Words

Can you match these words
to the pictures?

children

river

ring

dog

shook

black

brown

Tricky Words

These tricky words are in the story
you have just read. They cannot
be sounded out. Can you memorize
them and read them super fast?

some	out
were	what
one	when
do	
there	

A Winter Storm

Written by Monica Hughes
Illustrated by Ian Cunliffe

It was winter. The road had drifts on it when Cliff and Stella were off to visit Gran.

All of a sudden there was a storm.

We must not get stuck in this storm.

The children started to run.
Cliff fell down and hurt one of
his legs.

Just as they were at the end of the
tunnel, Stella got back with help.

What do you think Wowzer
did then?

He just shook himself and
then ran off!

Story Words

Can you match these words to the pictures?

leg

Cliff

Stella

Wowzer

jacket

MEET ALL THESE FRIENDS IN BUZZ BOOKS:

Thomas the Tank Engine
The Animals of Farthing Wood
James Bond Junior
Fireman Sam
Joshua Jones
Rupert
Babar

First published in Great Britain 1993 by Buzz Books,
an imprint of Reed Children's Books
Michelin House, 81 Fulham Road, London, SW3 6RB
and Auckland, Melbourne, Singapore and Toronto

ISBN 1 85591 317 8

Printed in Italy by Olivotto

RUPERT™
and the
CROCK OF GOLD

Story by Norman Redfern
Illustrations by SPJ Design

It was a sunny Saturday morning in
Nutwood. Rupert and his mother and
father were eating their breakfast.

"It's a lovely day today, Rupert," said
Mrs Bear. "Why don't you ask some of
your friends to a picnic on the fields?"

"Thanks, Mummy," said Rupert. "I'll ask
Bingo and Edward."

After breakfast, Rupert and his mother
began to prepare the picnic. Suddenly,
Rupert heard a clattering, pattering noise
from the garden. He looked out of the
kitchen window.

"Oh, no!" he cried in dismay. "It's pouring
with rain!"

"It's only an April shower," his mother
told him. "It won't last very long."

Sure enough, the shower passed quickly
and the sun shone through the clouds
once more.

Mrs Bear looked out of the window again.

"Just look at that!" she said.

In the sky was a perfect rainbow. The
colours were so bright and clear that
Rupert felt sure he could touch them.

8

"They say there's a crock of gold at the
end of every rainbow," said his mother.
"But no one can ever take any of it."

"Why can't they take the gold?" asked
Rupert. "What will happen?"

"It's a mystery," replied Mrs Bear. "If
anyone ever comes too close to the crock of
gold, the rainbow just vanishes!"

A good mystery, thought Rupert, is just what I need on a wet Saturday. He put on his coat and set off to meet his friends.

But when he turned the corner, he saw the rainbow again. It seemed to touch the ground just behind the tall pagoda where his friend the Chinese conjurer lived.

Rupert was determined to find the gold at the rainbow's end. When he came to the pagoda, Rupert began to run. I must hurry, he thought, before the rainbow vanishes. He rushed around the pagoda and raced to the spot where the rainbow touched the ground.

But the rainbow had disappeared.

Rupert stood by the pagoda, disappointed and out of breath.

"Training for school sports day, Rupert?"

Rupert turned round to see Tigerlily skipping down the path.

"No, I, um, oh, dear," he panted.

12

"So where were you going in such a hurry?" asked Tigerlily.

"Well, here, I think," he replied. "But when I got here, it wasn't here, and now I don't know where to go."

"What wasn't here?" frowned Tigerlily.

"The rainbow," sighed Rupert. "I thought that if I ran really fast, I could catch the end of the rainbow and see the crock of gold. But now it's gone. It must be magic!"

"Well, if it is magic," said Tigerlily, "we'll find a spell in one of Daddy's books."

"Shouldn't we ask your father first?" asked Rupert.

"He's busy," said Tigerlily quickly. "We'd better not disturb him."

Inside the pagoda, Tigerlily led Rupert to her father's library. She took a very old, very heavy book down from the shelf and laid it on her father's reading desk.

"Let's see," she said. "Clouds, gales, monsoons, rain — rainbows!"

Rupert leaned across to see what the book said. Behind him, a secret door opened.

"Helping Rupert with his homework, Tigerlily?" asked the Chinese conjurer.

Rupert and Tigerlily jumped up.

"No, no, just reading," said Tigerlily.

"Just reading my book of spells," said her father, looking very stern. "Why were you reading my book?"

Rupert took a deep breath, and told the conjurer about the rainbow.

"Do you really want to see the gold?" asked Tigerlily's father.

"Yes," answered Rupert.

"I do have a spell which will take you to the end of the rainbow," said the conjurer.

Tigerlily tugged at her father's sleeve.

"Oh Daddy," she cried. "Let me go too!"

"Very well, Tigerlily," said the Chinese conjurer. "But you must both promise me that you will not touch the gold."

"We promise," they said.

"Now, come out to the garden," said the conjurer.

Rupert and Tigerlily followed him outside.
In the garden, the conjurer uttered his
magic spell. Rupert looked up at the grey
sky. Slowly, it began to glow with bright,
clear colours.

"The rainbow!" he cried.

"Hold hands, please," said the conjurer.
"Walk straight ahead."

In front of them was a damp, foggy cloud.
Together, Rupert and Tigerlily walked
slowly into it.

18

"Where are we?" asked Tigerlily.

Rupert looked down. A fine mist swirled around his feet, then rose like a marvellous coloured fountain and curved away over their heads.

"We're at the end of the rainbow!" he gasped. "Look! Down there!"

At the very foot of the arch was a pot, just like the ones in his mother's larder. It was filled to the brim with the purest, most precious gold.

"Look at that!" cried Rupert. "Just wait till I
tell Bingo and Edward!"

Tigerlily bent over the crock.

"They'll never believe you," she said.

"I wouldn't make up a story like this,"
replied Rupert. "They know I wouldn't.
Come on, Tigerlily, I think it's time we
went back to Nutwood."

"All right," said Tigerlily, reluctantly. "Let's just have one more look at the rainbow first."

Rupert craned his neck to look up at the beautiful arch over their heads. Tigerlily watched him until she was sure he was looking the other way. Then she reached into the pot of gold.

"Ready?" asked Rupert. "Hold my hand."

They walked together back through the
cloud again. When the mist cleared, Rupert
looked around.

"That's funny," he said. "We haven't
arrived in your father's garden. We're on
Nutwood Common! Look! There's Bingo,
and Edward!"

"Rupert! Tigerlily!" cried Bingo. "Where
have you been?"

"I was just on my way to meet you,"
Rupert told his friends.

22

"Tigerlily and I have had a wonderful
adventure. We went to the end of the
rainbow. We've seen the crock of gold!"

Before Bingo or Edward could say a word,
Tigerlily rushed forward.

"I can prove it!" she said.

She reached inside her robe and pulled out something small and yellow. She held it under Bingo's nose.

"Look!" she said. "Real gold, from the rainbow's end!"

Bingo and Edward looked at Tigerlily's gold coin.

Suddenly, Rupert had a horrible, sinking feeling. His friends were laughing!

"Very good, Tigerlily!" chuckled Edward.

"It looks just like gold!" giggled Bingo.

"You must think we're April fools!"
laughed Edward.

Tigerlily looked at her piece of gold, and
saw that it wasn't gold at all. It was a
yellow pebble, as dull as any on the beach.

25

Rupert turned away. Standing quietly to one side, Tigerlily's father, the Chinese conjurer, was looking sterner than ever.

"I don't understand," said Rupert. "I saw real gold at the rainbow's end!"

"Your friends believed you until they saw Tigerlily's pebble," replied the conjurer. "Now they think it's just a joke."

"But it isn't!" cried Rupert.

"Tigerlily!" said the Chinese conjurer. "What did you promise?"

"I promised not to touch the gold," said his daughter, looking very ashamed.

"Yes, you did," said the conjurer. "Bingo! Edward! Do you know what there is at the rainbow's end?"

"A crock of gold!" they cried.

"You see?" asked the conjurer. "No need to prove it."

"I'm sorry, Daddy," said Tigerlily.

"So you should be, Tigerlily," replied her father. "For there is magic, too, at the rainbow's end."

"You were really there!" said Bingo.

"Yes, we really were," said Rupert. "Mind you, I prefer Nutwood."

"Why?" asked Edward, looking puzzled.

"I'd choose my friends over a crock of gold any day," he said, as it began to rain again.